KU-197-205

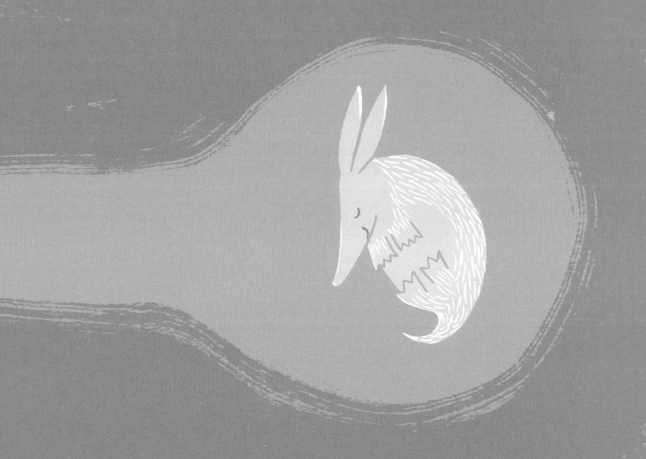

FOR MISHA AND KIYO,
THE AARDVARKS WHO INSPIRED THIS STORY.

First published 2019 by Two Hoots
This edition published 2020 by Two Hoots
an imprint of Pan Macmillan
The Smithson, 6 Briset Street, London, EC1M 5NR
Associated companies throughout the world
www.panmacmillan.com
ISBN 978-1-5098-4295-7
Text and illustrations copyright © Morag Hood 2019
Moral rights asserted.

All rights reserved. No part of this publication may be reproduced, stored in a retrieval system, or transmitted,
in any form or by any means (electronic, mechanical, photocopying, recording or otherwise),
without the prior written permission of the publisher.

1 3 5 7 9 8 6 4 2
A CIP catalogue record for this book is available from the British Library.
Printed in China
The illustrations in this book were painted in gouache and then digitally coloured.

www.twohootsbooks.com

AALFRED AND AALBERT

MORAG HOOD

TWO HOOTS

This is the story of two aardvarks.

I'm Aalfred,

thought Aalfred.

Aalfred loved stars,
broccoli and picnics.

Aalbert loved flowers, sunshine and cheese.

And they both loved sleeping
rather a lot, except . . .

Aalbert slept all night,

and Aalfred slept all day.

Which meant that they
had never met each other.

AALFRED'S
BURROW

AALBERT'S
BURROW

. . . or one of a two,

thought Aalbert.

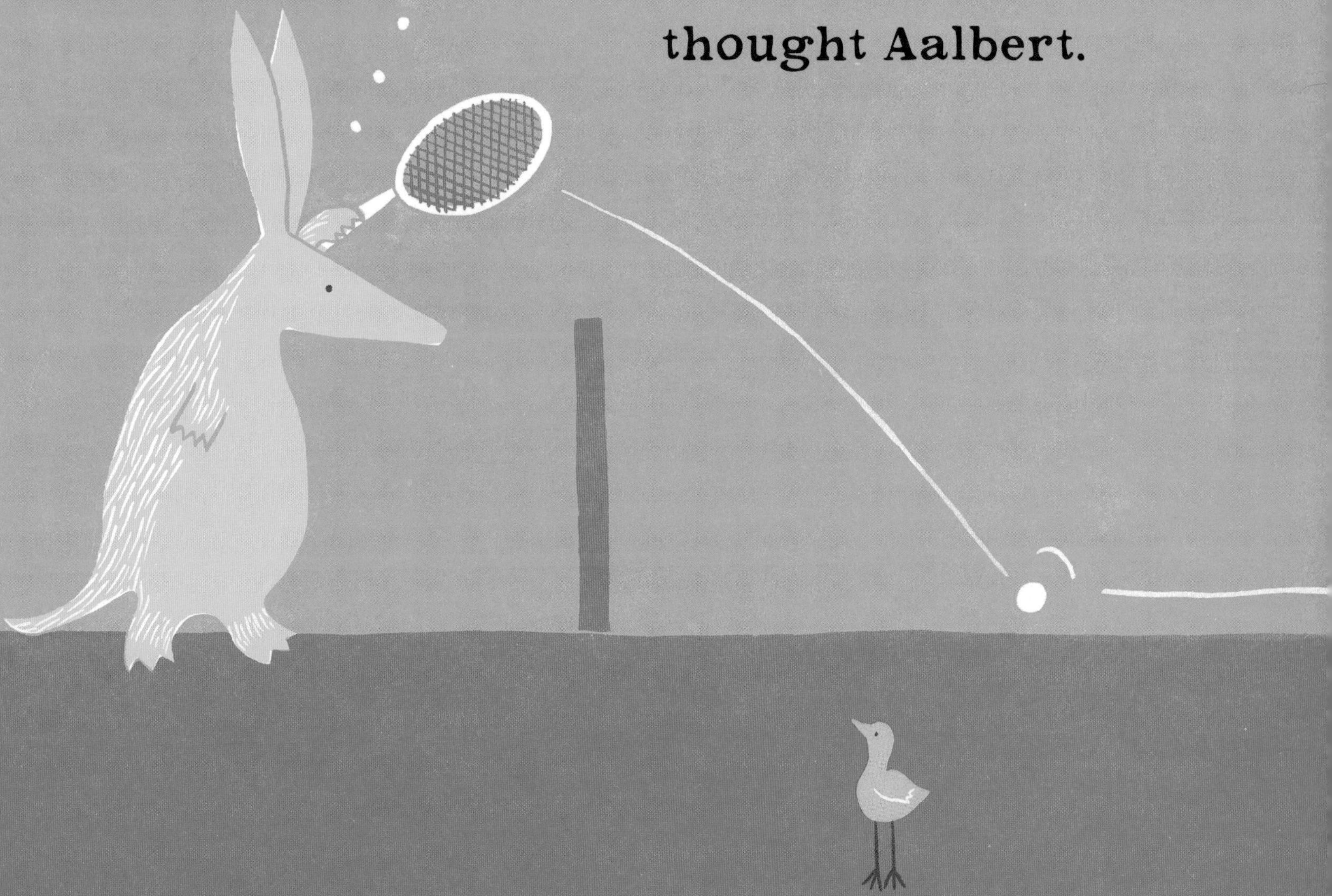

But most of the time their minds
were on other things.

And so it looked like nothing
would ever change.

Unless . . .

...somebody came up with a plan.

But nothing changed when Aalbert
was woken up one night.

thought Aalbert...

... before he turned over
and fell back to sleep.

Nothing changed when Aalfred saw something very unusual.

I wonder where that broccoli is going?

thought Aalfred ...

Nothing changed even when they both got in a bit of a tangle.

It seemed that nothing could bring
Aalfred and Aalbert together.

Nothing at all.

And that was very sad.

And,

in a way,

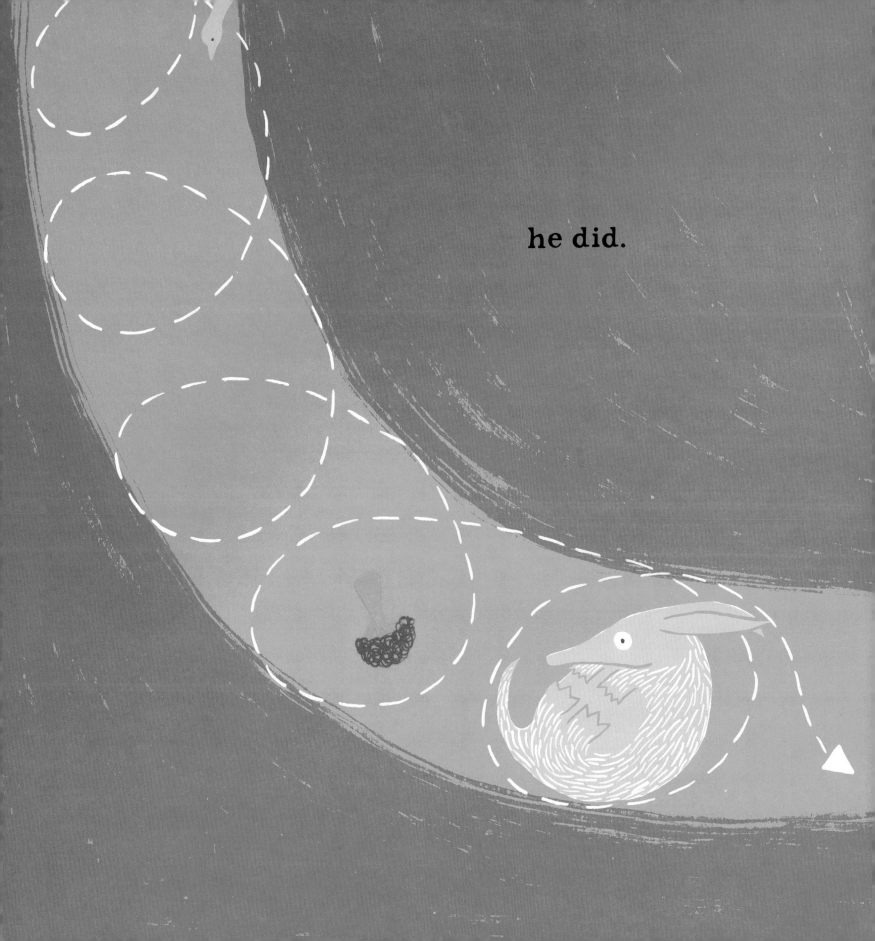

he did.

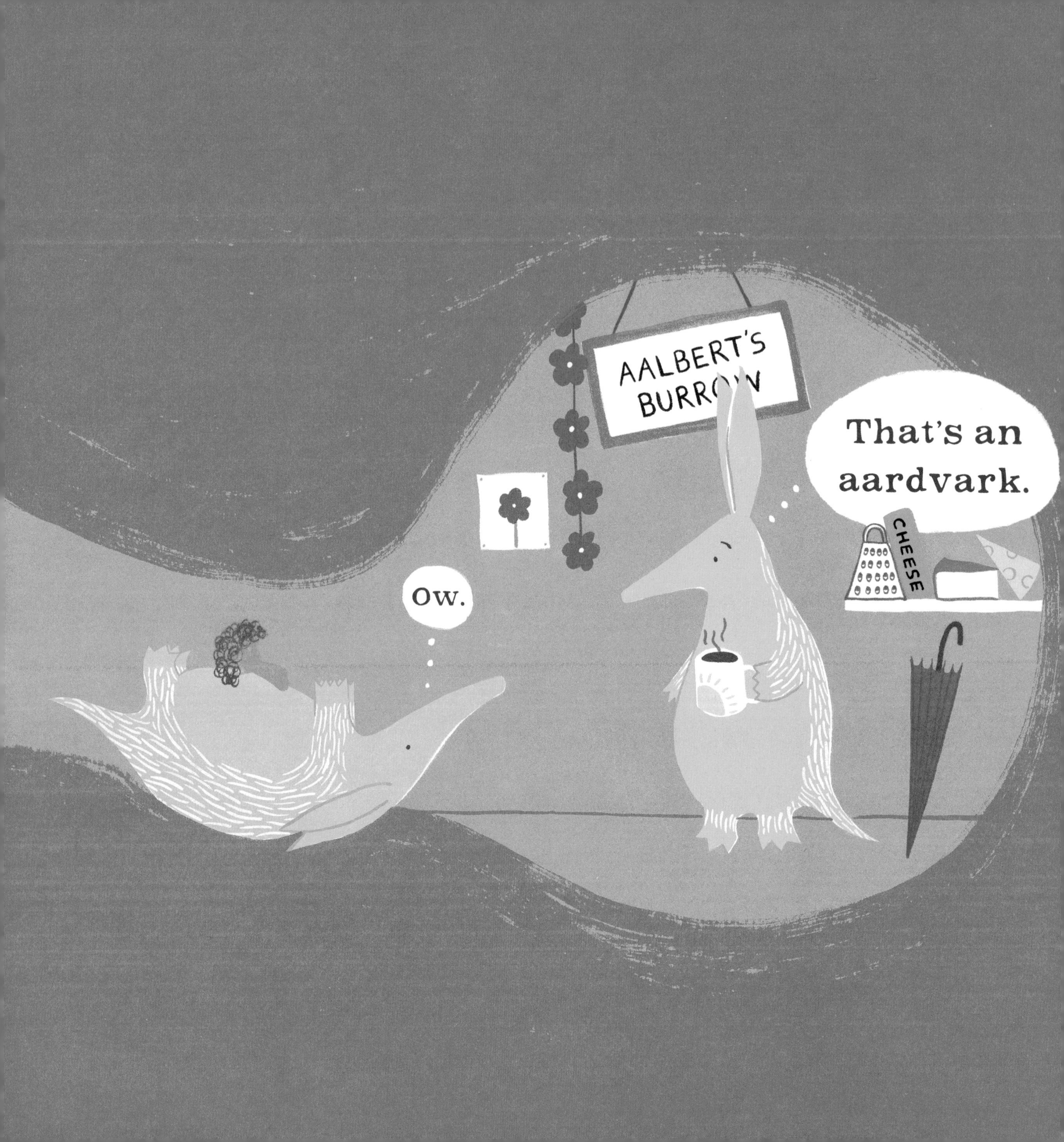
AALBERT'S
BURROW
That's an aardvark.
CHEESE
Ow.

Because that was the story of
how Aalfred met Aalbert . . .

And they all lived happily ever aafter.

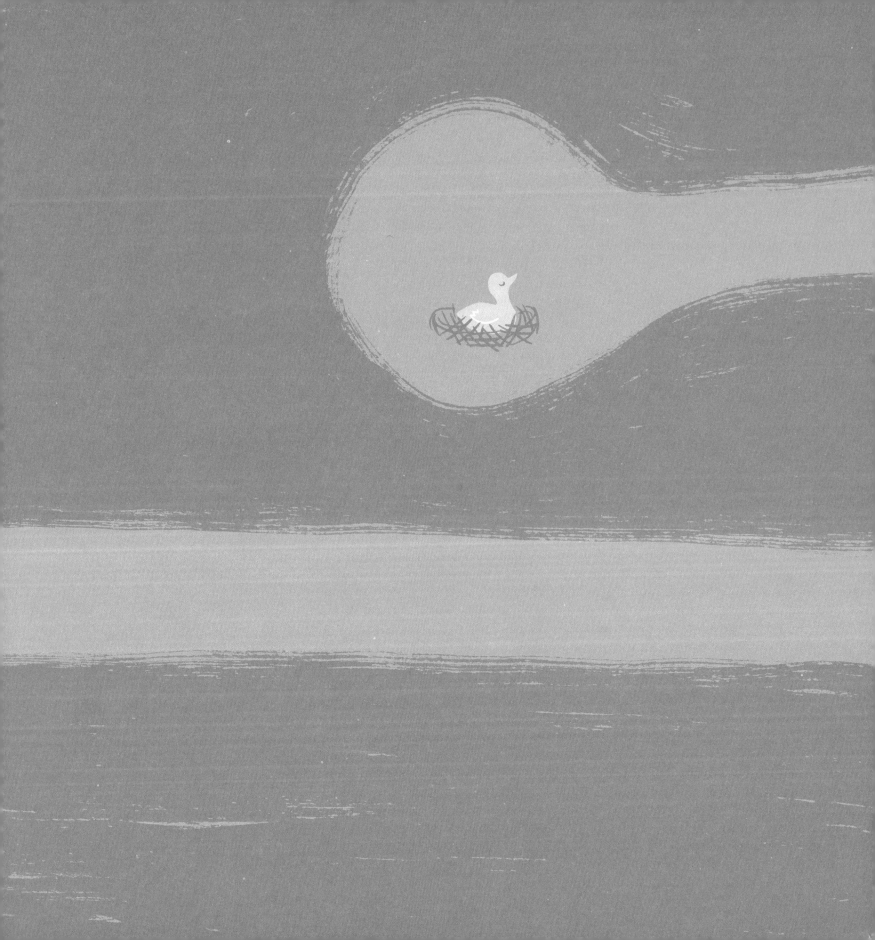

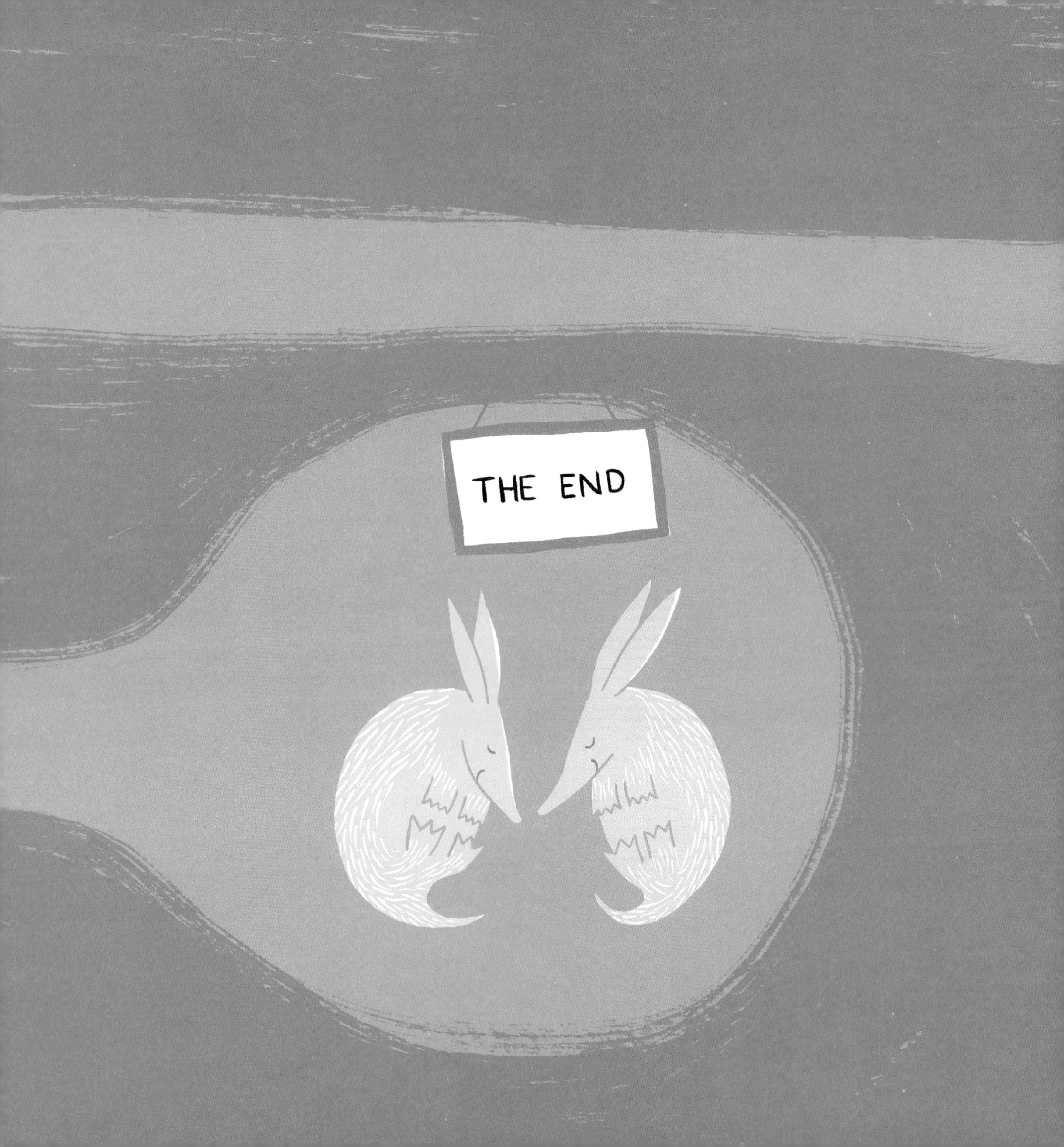
THE END

HERE ARE SOME FACTS ABOUT AARDVARKS

- The name Aardvark comes from the Afrikaans language and means "earth pig".

- During the day most aardvarks (except for Aalbert) spend their time sleeping in holes underground called burrows.

- Their claws look like small spades which make them powerful and speedy diggers. They can dig up to 60cm in 15 seconds!

- Aardvarks can close their nostrils to stop dust and tickly insects from getting in.